Here's what kids have to say about reading Magic Tree House® books and Magic Tree House® Merlin Missions:

Thank you for writing these great books! I have learned a great deal of information about history and the world around me.—Rosanna

Your series, the Magic Tree House, was really influential on my late childhood years. [Jack and Annie] taught me courage through their rigorous adventures and profound friendship, and how they stuck it out through thick and thin, from start to finish.—Joe

Your description is fantastic! The words pop out . . . oh, man . . . [the Magic Tree House series] is really exciting!—Christina

I like the Magic Tree House series. I stay up all night reading them. Even on school nights!—Peter

I think I've read about twenty-five of your Magic Tree House books! I'm reading every Magic Tree House book I can get my hands on!—Jack

Never stop writing, and if you can't think about anything to write about, don't worry, use some of my ideas!!—Kevin

Parents, teachers, and librarians love Magic Tree House® books, too!

[Magic Tree House] comes up quite a bit at parent/ teacher conferences.... The parents are amazed at how much more reading is being done at home because of your books. I am very pleased to know such fun and interesting reading exists for students.... Your books have also made students want to learn more about the places Jack and Annie visit. What wonderful starters for some research projects!—Kris L.

As a librarian, I have seen many happy young readers coming into the library to check out the next Magic Tree House book in the series. I have assisted young library patrons with finding nonfiction materials related to the Magic Tree House book they have read.... The message you are sending to children is invaluable: siblings can be friends; boys and girls can hang out together....—Lynne H.

[My daughter] had a slow start reading, but somehow with your Magic Tree House series, she has been inspired and motivated to read. It is with such urgency that she tracks down your books. She often blurts out various facts and lines followed by "I read that in my Magic Tree House book."—Jenny E.

[My students] seize every opportunity they can to reread a Magic Tree House book or look at all the wonderful illustrations. Jack and Annie have opened a door to a world of literacy that I know will continue throughout the lives of my students.—Deborah H.

[My son] carries his Magic Tree House books everywhere he goes. He just can't put the book he is reading down until he finishes it. . . . He is doing better in school overall since he has made reading a daily thing. He even has a bet going with his aunt that if he continues doing well in school, she will continue to buy him the next book in the Magic Tree House series.—Rosalie R.

MAGIC TREE HOUSE® #36
A MERLIN MISSION

Blizzard of the Blue Moon

by Mary Pope Osborne

illustrated by Sal Murdocca

A STEPPING STONE BOOK™

Random House 🏠 New York

Grateful acknowledgment is made to Pantheon Books, a division of Random House, Inc., for permission to reprint an excerpt from "The Unicorn in Captivity" from *The Unicorn and Other Poems* by Anne Morrow Lindbergh, copyright © 1956 by Anne Morrow Lindbergh, renewed 1984 by Anne Morrow Lindbergh. Reprinted by permission of Pantheon Books, a division of Random House, Inc.

Text copyright © 2006 by Mary Pope Osborne
Illustrations copyright © 2006 by Sal Murdocca
Window cling illustration copyright © 2006 by Sal Murdocca

www.randomhouse.com/kids
www.magictreehouse.com

Educators and librarians, for a variety of teaching tools, visit us at
www.randomhouse.com/teachers

Library of Congress Cataloging-in-Publication Data
Osborne, Mary Pope.
Blizzard of the blue moon / by Mary Pope Osborne ; illustrated by Sal Murdocca.
   p. cm. — (Magic tree house ; #36)
"A Merlin mission."
"A Stepping Stone book."
Summary: The magic tree house carries Jack and Annie to New York City in 1938 on a mission to rescue the last unicorn.
ISBN: 978-0-375-83037-2 (trade) — ISBN: 978-0-375-93037-9 (lib. bdg.) —
ISBN: 978-0-375-83038-9 (pbk.)
[1. Time travel—Fiction. 2. Magic—Fiction. 3. Unicorns—Fiction. 4. Depressions—1929—Fiction. 5. Tree houses—Fiction. 6. Brothers and sisters—Fiction. 7. New York (N.Y.)—History—1898–1951—Fiction.] I. Murdocca, Sal, ill. II. Title. III. Osborne, Mary Pope. Magic tree house series ; #36.
PZ7.O81167Bli 2006 [Fic]—dc22 2006001838

Printed in the United States of America
20 19 18

*To Elwood Smith, who long ago
in New York City inspired me
to write for children*

Dear Reader,

Finally Jack and Annie go to New York City, the place I called home for over twenty-five years. New York City is a larger-than-life place, filled with skyscrapers, taxis, subways, parks, museums, theaters, and busy, bustling streets. The city has all kinds of weather, too, from heat waves to raging snowstorms. I remember one particularly dramatic blizzard in 1996. The city came to a complete standstill as the wind howled and it snowed and snowed and snowed. When the storm finally ended, pale sunlight shone on all the white streets and sidewalks—and everyone went out to play. Kids made giant snowmen and dogs tunneled through the snowdrifts.

No matter what disasters it suffers, New York City always comes back. I hope you have a great adventure there with Jack and Annie.

Mary Pope Osborne

CONTENTS

He stays, the Unicorn,
In captivity. . . .
Yet look again—
His horn is free,
Rising above
Chain, fence, and tree.
—Anne Morrow Lindbergh,
"The Unicorn in Captivity"

Prologue

One summer day, a mysterious tree house appeared in the woods. A brother and sister named Jack and Annie soon learned that the tree house was magic—it could take them to any time and any place in history. They also learned that the tree house belonged to Morgan le Fay, a magical librarian from the legendary realm of Camelot.

After Jack and Annie traveled on many adventures for Morgan, Merlin the magician began sending them on "Merlin Missions" in the tree house. With help from two young sorcerers named Teddy and Kathleen, Jack and Annie visited four mythical places and found valuable objects to help save Camelot.

For their next four Merlin Missions, Jack and Annie were told they must travel to *real* times and *real* places in history and prove to Merlin that they could use magic wisely. First they went on a mission to the city of Venice. Next they journeyed to the ancient city of Baghdad. On their most recent trip they visited the city of Paris in 1889. Now they are waiting to hear from Merlin again. . . .

CHAPTER ONE

The Last Unicorn

The November sky was gray with clouds. Jack sat reading in front of the living room fire.

"Who wants hot chocolate?" his dad called from the kitchen.

"Me, please!" said Jack.

The front door burst open, and with a gust of cold wind, Annie rushed inside. "Jack! Guess what!" she whispered. "It's back!"

"How do you know?" said Jack.

"I was walking home from the library"— Annie paused to catch her breath—"and I saw a flash in the sky above the woods. The last time that happened—"

Before she could finish the sentence, Jack jumped up. "Dad, Annie and I are going to go outside for a while!" he shouted. "Can the hot chocolate wait till we get back?"

"Sure, have fun!" their dad called from the kitchen.

"I have to get my pack," Jack said to Annie. "Meet you on the porch."

"Don't forget the rhyme book!" said Annie.

Annie slipped outside and Jack ran up to his room. He grabbed his backpack. He checked to make sure their book of magic rhymes was inside. *Good*, there it was.

Jack charged back downstairs. He pulled on his boots, put on his jacket, tied a scarf around his neck, grabbed his mittens, and headed out the door.

"Come on!" said Annie.

Jack could see his breath in the cold air. "Brrr," he said. "Let's hurry!"

Jack and Annie ran down the street and into the Frog Creek woods. They wove between the trees, their boots crunching through the fallen leaves.

Jack stopped. The magic tree house *was* back. High in a tall oak tree, it was silhouetted against the gray November sky. "You were right," he said to Annie. "Good work."

"Thanks," Annie said. She ran to the rope ladder and started up. Jack followed her.

When they climbed inside the tree house, Jack and Annie saw a book and a scroll of parchment paper lying on the floor. Annie picked up the scroll, unrolled it, and read aloud.

Dear Jack and Annie of Frog Creek,

I am sending you on one more mission to prove that you can use magic wisely. This poem will guide you.

—M.

The very last unicorn
Is now hidden well
By those who have put him
Under a spell.

Four centuries, four decades
From that afternoon,
At the end of November,
Before the blue moon,

He will wake once more
And be free to go home
If you call out his name:
Divine Flower of Rome.

You must coax him to stand
Once his name is spoken.

*His chain will break
And the spell, too, be broken.*

*Then a young girl must love him
And show him the way,
Lest he be trapped forever
On public display.*

*If he loses this chance
To rise and depart,
All magic will fade
From his horn and his heart.*

"A unicorn!" breathed Annie. "I love him already. *I'll* show him the way!"

"But this poem is really hard to understand," said Jack. "What kind of research book did Morgan send us?"

He picked up the book that had been left for them by Morgan le Fay, the librarian of Camelot. The cover showed a row of skyscrapers. The title was *New York City Guide Book, 1938.*

"New York City?" said Annie. "I love New

York City! Remember the great time we had there with Aunt Mallory?"

"Yeah, I love it, too," said Jack. "But why would there be a unicorn in New York City in 1938? A unicorn is an ancient fantasy creature. New York City's a real place, and 1938 is not even that long ago."

"You're right," said Annie. "It sounds like a hard mission. But don't forget we have Teddy and Kathleen's magic rhymes to help us."

"Yeah," said Jack. He pulled out the book

given to them by their friends Teddy and Kathleen, two young enchanters of Camelot. "The problem is, we can only use each rhyme once, and we've already used seven out of the ten."

"Which means we still have three left," said Annie. "What are they?"

"Pull a Cloud from the Sky," said Jack.

"Cool," said Annie.

"Yeah, it is," said Jack. "But I'm not sure it will be much use." He looked back at the book. *"Find a Treasure You Must Never Lose,"* he said.

"Hey, that's a really good one!" said Annie. "The unicorn's a treasure. So that rhyme could take care of our whole mission."

"But it only *partly* fits," said Jack. "You could call the unicorn a treasure. But once we find him, we *have* to lose him. He has to go back home."

"Oh, right . . . ," said Annie. "What else?"

"Your favorite," said Jack. *"Turn into Ducks."*

Annie laughed. "I can't wait to use that one!" she said.

"I hope we *never* use that one," said Jack. He didn't want to waddle around and quack like a duck. "These leftover rhymes don't seem very helpful to me."

"Well, let's just wait and see," said Annie. "But now . . ." She held up Morgan's research book and smiled.

Jack nodded. "New York City, here we come," he said. He pointed at the book's cover. "I wish we could go *there!*"

The wind started to blow.

The tree house started to spin.

It spun faster and faster.

Then everything was still.

Absolutely still.

CHAPTER TWO

Who Are They?

Snow blew into the tree house.

Jack and Annie wore wool coats, hats, and mittens. Jack's canvas backpack had turned into a leather briefcase with buckles and a shoulder strap. Jack and Annie looked out the window.

Below the tree house was a wide, snow-covered field that ended in a wall of evergreen trees. Beyond the trees was a city skyline.

"This is definitely New York," said Annie. "See the Empire State Building? Remember our visit to the top?" She pointed to a faraway building

that rose above the others. "This must be Central Park. I remember that big field."

"Yeah, I do, too," said Jack. "But we've landed in New York in 1938. It was different back then." He opened their research book and read from the introduction:

> The city of New York is the largest city in the Western Hemisphere. It covers an area of 322 square miles.

Jack closed the book. "Whoa. Even in 1938, New York was a huge city," he said. "This is going to be like looking for a needle in a haystack."

"I'll read our mission poem again," said Annie. She read the first verse aloud:

> *The very last unicorn*
> *Is now hidden well*
> *By those who have put him*
> *Under a spell.*

"Okay, so this unicorn was put under a spell," said Jack, "and he must be hidden somewhere in New York, or Merlin wouldn't have sent us here."

"Right," said Annie. She read the next verse:

> *Four centuries, four decades*
> *From that afternoon,*
> *At the end of November,*
> *Before the blue moon,*

"What's a blue moon?" asked Annie, looking up. "I've heard that expression before."

"It's when you have two full moons in the same month," said Jack. "It doesn't happen very often."

"Oh," said Annie. She read on:

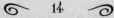

He will wake once more
And be free to go home
If you call out his name:
Divine Flower of Rome.

"Wait, does that mean the unicorn's name is Divine Flower of Rome?" asked Jack.

"I guess," said Annie. She read on:

You must coax him to stand
Once his name is spoken.
His chain will break
And the spell, too, be broken.

Then a young girl must love him
And show him the way,
Lest he be trapped forever
On public display.

If he loses this chance
To rise and depart,
All magic will fade
From his horn and his heart.

"So *I'm* the young girl!" said Annie. "And I

have to help him get home, or his magic will fade away forever!"

"Right," said Jack. "Okay. Let's review: There's a unicorn on public display somewhere in New York City. He's under a spell. The spell runs out in late November before a blue moon. But he'll only wake up when someone calls his name, which is *Divine Flower of Rome.* Then a young girl—*you*—must love him and show him the way home."

"Great," said Annie. "Let's get started."

"Get started? *How?*" said Jack.

"Maybe we should talk to some New Yorkers," said Annie. "We can ask them if they know anything about a unicorn in New York City." She looked out the window. "There're some people in the park right now."

Jack looked out. Through the falling snow, he saw girls crossing the field carrying skates. He saw two people standing on top of a small hill. One wore a cape, and the other a long raincoat.

"If we start asking people about unicorns, they'll think we're crazy," said Jack.

"Who cares?" said Annie. "Maybe *someone* will at least know *something* that can help us. Let's go down." She started down the ladder.

Jack quickly packed up their books. He buckled his bag and followed her. When they stepped onto the ground, Jack and Annie looked around. The skaters were gone. The two people on the hill were gone, too.

"Where'd everybody go?" said Jack.

"I don't know. But we'll find someone else. Come on," said Annie.

Jack and Annie started across the wide field. The snow was falling fast and furiously. The wind blew harder.

"Look, a frozen pond," said Annie, pointing. "That must be where the skaters were coming from."

Wet snow stuck to Jack's glasses. He wiped them off so he could see. No one was skating on the pond now. Whirlwinds of powdery snow swirled over the ice.

"Keep going," said Jack.

They kept trudging through the snow.

"Hey, look! Remember that?" said Annie.

"What?" said Jack. He wiped the snow off his glasses again. He saw a merry-go-round. "Oh, yeah." On their trip to New York with their aunt Mallory, they'd taken a ride on it. But now the riderless painted horses looked sad and lonely.

"I feel like we're the last living creatures in Central Park," said Jack.

"Which way do we go now?" asked Annie. "Which way did we come from?"

It was hard to see anything in the white haze of the falling snow. The buildings bordering the park and the skyscrapers in the distance had disappeared.

"Let's see what our book says," said Jack. He unbuckled his leather briefcase and pulled out their research book. He found a picture of Central Park and read:

> **Central Park is a vast natural area in the middle of New York City. The park has thirty-two miles of winding foot-paths and covers 840 acres of land. It has rock formations, woods, and many bodies of water. It also has—**

"Okay, okay, got it," said Annie. "It's a *big* park. Is there a map that shows where we are?"

Jack tried to read from the index, but the wind and snow made it impossible. He stuffed the book back into his briefcase. "Forget it," he said. "Let's just try to get out of the park."

Jack and Annie turned away from the lonely merry-go-round and walked across the snow. A gust of wind blew Jack's cap off. As he turned around to grab it, he saw a couple walking a short distance behind them.

The two people looked like teenagers. They were walking with their heads bowed against the wind. The girl wore a dark cape with a hood. The boy wore a hat and a tan raincoat with a belt.

"Hey, look—" Jack said to Annie. But at that moment, the wind shook the trees, and big clumps of snow fell from the branches. Jack and Annie ducked and covered their heads. When the wind died down, Jack looked around for the couple.

"They're gone now," he said.

"*Who's* gone?" said Annie. "Who did you see?"

"Two teenagers, I think," said Jack. "A boy and a girl. We saw them earlier from the tree house. I think they might be following us."

"Wait a second," said Annie. "Two teenagers? A boy and a girl? Following us? Who does that remind you of?"

A big smile crossed Jack's face. "Teddy and Kathleen?" he said.

"Think about it," said Annie. "On our last three missions, it seemed like Teddy and

Kathleen were always nearby, wearing disguises, ready to help us when we needed it."

"Right," said Jack. "We could sure use their help now." He turned around. "Hello!" he shouted.

"Hello!" Annie yelled.

But the wind answered them with a howl. More clumps of snow blew down on Jack and Annie.

"Let's get going," said Annie. "They'll find us sooner or later. They always do."

CHAPTER THREE

Lost in Central Park

Jack and Annie kept walking until they came to the ice pond again. "We've been here before," said Jack. "We're going in circles. How do we get out of the park?"

"We have to try to walk in a straight line," said Annie.

Annie and Jack struggled on. Jack kept looking back, trying to catch sight of Teddy and Kathleen again. But it was getting harder and harder to see anything. Wet snow kept sticking to his glasses. Snow had blown up the sleeves of his jacket, under his neck scarf, and into his mittens.

"Yikes!" said Annie. She grabbed Jack's arm. "Look!"

A huge wolf-like dog stood on a ledge above them, his mouth open.

"Whoa!" said Jack.

The dog didn't move. He stood perfectly still.

Annie laughed. "Oh, he's a statue!" she said. She ran to a plaque under the dog statue, brushed off the snow, and shouted to Jack. "His name is Balto! In 1925, he carried medicine six hundred miles through a blizzard in Alaska!"

"That's really great," said Jack. "But how do we get out of the park?"

"Well, if we follow this path, it's bound to lead somewhere," said Annie.

Jack followed Annie up a wide path. They walked and walked, passing a snow-covered outdoor stage and a fountain with the statue of an angel. Raising her outspread wings, the angel seemed about to fly away.

"Which way now?" said Jack.

Two paths led away from the angel fountain: one to the right, one to the left. "I don't know," said Annie. "Pick one."

Jack headed to the left. Annie followed. They passed a frozen lake and walked over an arched bridge. Jack kept his eyes on the ground and walked and walked and walked. Every time he lifted his head, the snow felt like needles against his skin.

Jack tried to keep walking in a straight line, but the path they were following began twisting and turning like a maze. Different paths branched off, curving this way and that. Jack remembered information from their research book: *The park has thirty-two miles of winding footpaths.*

"We have *got* to get off these paths!" he shouted to Annie. "Or we'll be lost in Central Park forever!"

Annie didn't answer. "Annie!" Jack shielded his face from the cutting wind and looked back. He didn't see her.

Jack turned around and around, looking for Annie. But he couldn't see anything—the world was completely white.

"Annie!" he cried. Had she gone off on another path? Was she lost? "Annie!"

She could wander around in the storm for

hours! thought Jack. *She could freeze to death! I have to find her!*

Jack tried to stay calm. He took a few breaths. *A rhyme,* he thought. He couldn't remember which magic rhymes were left. He struggled to unbuckle his briefcase—his fingers felt frozen. He pulled out the book and hunched over it, trying to shelter it from the storm. He wiped his glasses off and read: *Turn into Ducks.* That wouldn't help. *Pull a Cloud from the Sky.* That would only make things worse. *Find a Treasure You Must Never Lose.*

Is Annie a treasure? Jack wondered. He'd always thought of a "treasure" as something super valuable, like gold or silver or rare jewels. But right now Annie seemed more valuable than any of those things. She seemed like the most valuable thing in the world. Jack found the rhyme and shouted:

Treasure forever must never be lost!
Um-motta cal, um-motta bost!

"Jack!"

Jack whirled around. Annie was standing right behind him. "There you are," she said. "I was afraid you got lost."

"*I* wasn't lost," said Jack. "*You* were lost." He slipped the rhyme book back into his briefcase.

"Not me, *you*," said Annie.

"Whatever," said Jack. "Just stay near me now." He took her hand and gripped it tightly. "Okay, let's figure out what to do."

"Wait, is that a castle over there?" said Annie.

"A *what*?" said Jack.

"A castle. Look!"

Peering through the storm, Jack saw a small castle sitting on top of a snowy hill. A light burned in a window.

"A castle in Central Park?" Jack said. "That's weird."

"Let's go see if anyone's inside," said Annie. "Maybe they can help us. People in a castle might know about unicorns."

"Or at least know how to get out of the park," said Jack.

Jack and Annie struggled up the stone steps that led to the castle. At the top of the steps, Jack glanced back at the park. He could barely make out two figures in the snow: one in a dark cape and one in a raincoat.

"Them—it's them!" said Jack.

A cloud of wind-driven snow blew over the couple. Jack kept looking, eager for another glimpse of the two young enchanters. But the snow hid everything in sight.

"They'll find us," said Annie. "Come on." She pushed open the door to the castle and led the way inside.

The door slammed shut behind them. Jack and Annie stood in a dimly lit hallway.

"Hello? Who's there?" a man called.

"Jack and Annie!" shouted Annie.

A tall, thin man came down a curving stone stairway. He wore an old-fashioned blue-striped suit. "Goodness! Two children!" he said. "What are you doing here on a day like today?"

"We got lost in the park," said Jack. "My

name's Jack and this is my sister, Annie."

"Pleased to meet you. I'm Bill Perkins," said the man. "Welcome to Belvedere Castle."

"What *is* this place?" asked Annie.

"The castle was built in 1869," said Mr. Perkins. "It was meant to be a delightful surprise when one wandered the park. Today it's a delightful surprise with a nature observatory and weather instruments inside."

"Weather instruments?" said Jack.

"Yes. I've come from the U.S. Weather Bureau to check them," said Mr. Perkins. "I'm afraid right now our data is telling us that the weather's undergoing a rapid and terrible change."

Jack shivered in his damp clothes. "Our data is telling us the same thing," he said.

"A storm has blown in from the Midwest, bringing wind and snow," said Mr. Perkins. "But after nightfall, things will get worse. Another storm is coming up from the South, gathering speed on its way."

"That sounds serious," said Annie.

"It's worse than serious," Mr. Perkins said. "It's disastrous. After dark, the two systems will meet and create a monster blizzard! It could be the worst in New York history! Even worse than the Blizzard of '88!"

Jack caught his breath.

"Poor New York," said Annie.

"Ah, yes, it's the last thing our great city needs during these hard times," said Mr. Perkins, shaking his head.

"Excuse me, but I have a question," said Annie. "Do you know if there's a full moon tonight?"

"Well, yes, there is," said Bill Perkins. "You won't see it, though—not through those storm clouds. Actually, it'll be the second full moon this month."

"*A blue moon!*" said Annie.

"You're exactly right, a blue moon indeed," said Mr. Perkins.

"I have another question," said Annie. "Do you know where we can find—"

"Um—any unusual animals?" Jack interrupted. "On public display somewhere? In New York City?"

"Well, your best bet in New York would be the Bronx Zoo," said Mr. Perkins. "They display all kinds of animals from all over the world."

"Great!" said Annie. "How do we get there?"

"What? You can't go to the zoo today!" said Mr. Perkins. "Not in this storm!"

"No, no, of course not," Jack said quickly. "But if we ever decide to go to the zoo—in the future—how would we get there?"

"Well, the best way would be to take the West Side IRT," said Mr. Perkins.

"What's that?" said Jack.

"A subway line that runs up the West Side," said Mr. Perkins. "The number two train on that line will take you to the Bronx Zoo."

"Oh, great, thanks for everything," said Jack. "We'd better get going now." He and Annie started toward the door.

"Wait, there's a telephone upstairs. Let me

ring up your parents. Perhaps they can come get you," said Mr. Perkins.

"Um, well," said Annie. "We—uh—we haven't lived here very long, and we don't have a telephone yet."

"She's right," said Jack. "But it's not far to where we live. We just need to get out of the park to the street."

"To the West Side!" said Annie.

"Yeah, yeah, the West Side," said Jack. "Can you tell us how to get there from here?"

"Certainly!" Mr. Perkins opened the door. Wind and snow blasted inside as he pointed to the right. "Cross the terrace and then walk down the stairs to a path. That path will take you out of the park to Eighty-first Street," he said. "Hurry home now!"

"We will!" said Jack.

"Thanks a lot, Mr. Perkins!" said Annie. And she and Jack headed back out into the blizzard.

CHAPTER FOUR

Hard Times

The wind lashed the bare trees and swept the snow into tall drifts. "That way!" said Annie. She led the way down the castle steps to the path.

"Mr. Perkins was a nice guy," said Annie as they headed toward the west side of the park.

"Yeah," said Jack. "Someday I'd like to go back there and see all his weather instruments."

Jack and Annie trudged through the storm, until they saw buildings just beyond the trees.

"We're almost out of Central Park!" Annie said.

Jack looked around. "Do you see Teddy and Kathleen?" he said.

"No, but we'd better keep going if we want to get to the zoo today," said Annie.

Jack agreed. Mr. Perkins had said that the blizzard was going to turn into a monster after dark. And dark came early in November.

They left the park and came to a wide city street. All sorts of things were blowing about in the wind: newspapers, hats, and umbrellas turned inside out. Jack and Annie grabbed a lamppost and clung to it, trying to keep from getting blown away, too. When there was a lull in the storm, they trudged across the avenue. It was lined with cars half buried in the snow.

Jack and Annie started down a side street. They passed an old man and woman huddled in a doorway, wrapped in torn blankets, burning a fire in a small stove. They passed a line of men dressed in ragged clothes standing outside a building. A sign said "Free Soup."

Jack hoped everyone outside would find better shelter before the monster blizzard hit.

"Excuse me!" Annie called to the men in the line for free soup. "Do you know where the West Side IRT subway is?"

"Two blocks!" said a man. "Keep going!"

"Thanks!" said Annie.

Jack and Annie kept going. They passed a firehouse, a cheese store, and a newsstand. Everything was closed and shuttered. Peddlers' carts were stuck in drifts.

Signs banged in the wind. One said:

MEATBALLS AND BEANS—10 CENTS!

Another said:

ZITO'S BAKERY—5 CENTS A LOAF!

A third said:

Lodging—2 dollars a week!

Jack and Annie crossed the street. They saw newsboys huddled under a theater awning. The boys had wrapped their feet and legs in newspapers to keep warm.

"Excuse me, where's the subway?" Jack shouted.

"End of the block and around the corner! Green ball!" said a boy.

Green ball? wondered Jack. *What does that mean?*

"Thanks!" said Annie. "You guys should go home! After dark, the storm's turning into a monster!"

Jack and Annie trudged on. When they turned the corner, Annie shouted, "Look! A green ball!"

On top of a post was a large green ball. The post was next to a stairway that led underground. A sign said:

UPTOWN IRT TRAINS, 1, 2, 3

"That's it! Mr. Perkins said we take the number two!" said Annie.

"Wait, do you see Teddy and Kathleen?" said Jack, peering through the snow. Annie looked with him down the city street.

"I don't see them. But I'm sure they'll find

us," said Annie. She and Jack started down the stairs that led underground. The stairway was filled with people trying to get out of the storm. Jack and Annie walked with the crowd into the subway station.

A long line waited in front of a turnstile. A sign over the turnstile said:

SUBWAY: 5¢

"Oops, do you have any money for the subway?" Annie asked Jack.

"Yeah, I think I left home with at least a dollar in change," said Jack. He reached into his pocket and pulled out two nickels.

"Cool," said Annie. She led the way to the line.

As they waited, Jack looked around the station. A banjo player played a silly tune, but no one smiled. A man in rags walked around, holding out a hat, begging for money. Jack took another nickel from his pocket and dropped it into the hat.

"Thank you, thank you. Bless you," said the beggar.

"Sure," said Jack.

As the beggar walked on, Jack looked at Annie. "Boy, just a little nickel made him so happy," he said.

"I know. Everyone seems really poor and desperate here," said Annie.

"I wonder why," said Jack. While the line moved slowly toward the turnstile, he pulled out their research book. He read aloud from the introduction:

> **In the 1930s, New York City, as well as the rest of the United States, suffered through hard times known as the Great Depression. Jobs were scarce, and many people had no money or homes.**

"That's what Mr. Perkins was talking about," said Jack. "Hard times."

"I wish we could help everyone," said Annie.

"Me too," said Jack.

"But right now our mission is to save a unicorn under a spell," said Annie.

Jack frowned. "Our mission sounds like a fairy tale from a make-believe world," he said. "Not the real world of the Great Depression."

"I know," said Annie. "Hey, it's almost our turn. What do we do?"

"Let's watch the person in front of us," said Jack.

Jack and Annie watched an old woman put her nickel in the slot of the turnstile, which led to the train platform. The woman pushed through and joined the crowd of people waiting for the train. Jack and Annie put their nickels into the slot and pushed through, too.

The platform was bitterly cold. People looked worried, as if they feared the subway train might never come. Jack felt worried, too, but mainly because their mission wasn't making any sense. They were trying to get to the zoo before the blue moon, *and* before a monster blizzard hit the city. But when they got to the zoo, what then?

"This is what I don't understand," Jack said to Annie. "The poem says the unicorn is on public display. But if that's true, why haven't we ever read about New York City once having a unicorn in a zoo? That would be major news."

"Yeah, but remember the poem says he's 'hidden well,' and he's 'under a spell,'" said Annie. "So maybe the spell makes him look like a regular animal. But when we get to the zoo and say his name, he'll come out of hiding and—and—"

"Reveal his true nature?" said Jack.

"Exactly!" said Annie.

"Okay . . . ," said Jack. "But how will we know what kind of animal to look for?"

A signal bell clanged. Lights appeared at the end of the tunnel. Jack and Annie moved with the crowd as it surged forward.

The subway train rumbled down the tracks. On the side of the train, Jack saw a big number 2. "That's us!" he said.

When the train stopped, everyone on the platform crammed inside. Jack and Annie were squashed into one of the first cars. All the seats were taken, so they had to stand in the aisle. They held on to a silver pole as more riders squeezed into the subway car and grabbed straps hanging overhead. Jack actually didn't mind the tight squeeze. He was anxious to thaw out from the cold.

"Look, Jack!" cried Annie. She pointed out a window of the subway car.

Jack peered out the window, just in time to see two people rush across the platform toward one of the rear cars. One was dressed in a dark cape, the other in a tan raincoat.

A bell sounded. The subway doors closed and the train started down the tracks.

"Yay! They're on the train!" exclaimed Annie.

"Cool," said Jack, grinning. "We'll see them when we get off."

"Hey, *where* do we get off?" said Annie.

"Oh, man, we forgot to ask!" said Jack. He turned to the lady next to them.

"Excuse me, where do we get off for the Bronx Zoo?" he asked her.

"Tremont Avenue," the woman said gruffly.

"Where's that?" asked Annie.

"There's a map," said the woman. She pointed to a map on the wall above a row of seated passengers.

Jack and Annie stared at all the colorful lines that showed the subway system. "Nothing here makes sense," said Jack.

"Do you need help?" the girl sitting under the map said. She wore a tattered purple shawl over her head and shoulders.

"Yes, please," said Annie. "Can you tell us where we get off for the Bronx Zoo?"

"It's much further north," said the girl. "I'll let you know when we get to the right stop."

"Thanks," said Jack.

The train bumped and creaked along,

stopping every couple of minutes. Jack looked out the window and tried to read the name of each station, but sometimes the platforms were too crowded. He was glad the girl in the shawl had promised to help them.

Just when Jack was starting to feel warm and a little drowsy, the girl called out, "Your stop's next!"

"Thanks a lot!" said Annie. She and Jack squeezed through the crowd toward the doors. When the train stopped and the doors opened, Jack and Annie were practically pushed out onto the platform with the other people leaving.

The subway doors closed and the train moved on.

CHAPTER FIVE

The Cloisters

"Do you see Teddy and Kathleen?" asked Jack.

The crowd was swarming away from the subway platform toward different exits. Jack couldn't see anyone who looked like the two young enchanters.

"No," said Annie. "But if we figured out where to get off, I'm sure they did, too. Let's hurry and get to the zoo. We can meet up with them there."

Jack and Annie moved with the crowd. They passed a change booth on the way out of the station. "Wait, I'll ask where to go," said Annie. She waited in line and then leaned forward to talk to the man in the booth. "Do you know how to walk to the Bronx Zoo from here?" she said.

"*Walk* to the Bronx Zoo? Are you out of your mind?" said the man. "This isn't the stop for the Bronx Zoo! It's much further north."

"You mean we got out at the wrong stop?" said Annie.

"You did, but it doesn't matter," said the man. "You can't get there now, anyway. The tracks near the zoo are above ground. And I just got word they're buried in snow."

"Oh, no," said Jack.

"Lousy day for the zoo, anyway," said the man. "Next!"

Jack and Annie stepped away from the booth and walked out of the subway station. The sidewalk was deserted. "Oh, man, that girl gave us the wrong information," said Jack.

"This is terrible," said Annie.

"No kidding," said Jack. He looked around, wondering what to do next.

AH-U-GA! AH-U-GA!

"What's that?" said Jack.

"It looks like a taxi." Annie pointed at a big yellow car with a checkerboard stripe and writing on the side. Its horn let out a loud squawk: *AH-U-GA! AH-U-GA!*

The driver stuck his head out the window. He wore a big furry cap that came down over his ears. "Need a taxi?" he called.

"Yes!" shouted Annie. "Come on, Jack! He can take us to the zoo!" Jack hurried after her through the snow.

The taxi driver stepped out of the cab and opened the back door. "Hop in!" he said. His cheerful voice was muffled through a plaid scarf that covered half his face.

"Thanks!" said Jack. He stepped onto a running board and then climbed inside.

The taxi was very roomy. Jack could stretch his legs out and not even touch the front seat. "Boy, lots more room in old cars than ours," he said to Annie.

"Yeah," said Annie. "And there's no seat belts."

"Oh, yeah," said Jack. "I guess old cars didn't have any. I hope this guy is a good driver."

The driver slid open a little window that separated the front seat from the back. "Where to?" he asked.

"Can you please take us to the Bronx Zoo?" said Annie.

"We're in a big hurry to get there," said Jack.

"Sure thing, kiddos," said the driver.

"Great," said Jack.

"Oh, how much will it cost?" asked Annie.

"About thirty cents," said the driver. "Can you afford it?"

"Sure thing, kiddo," said Annie.

The driver laughed and closed the window.

Then the taxi began moving through the snow.

"Everything's so cheap here," Annie said to Jack.

"To *us* it is," said Jack. "But it's the Great Depression. Lots of people don't even have a nickel."

The taxi slid over the icy road and bumped over the curb. "Whoa!" said Jack, slipping off the seat.

"Sorry, kiddos!" called the driver. He got the taxi back onto the street. Then he plowed on through the snow, swerving this way and that.

The ride seemed dangerous in the bad weather, but Jack didn't want to get out now. He stared nervously out the window. The streets were empty of people. All the stores were closed and shuttered. Snow was piling up on apartment stoops, fire escapes, and iron balconies. Many of the buildings were shabby and crumbling, with broken windows.

"Hard times," Annie said softly.

"Yep," said Jack. He took a deep breath.

The taxi climbed up a road lined with tall evergreen trees. Suddenly it skidded and came to a stop. The engine roared, but the taxi's wheels only spun in the snow.

"What's happening?" Jack wondered aloud. He tapped on the glass that separated them from the driver.

The driver slid the window open. "Too bad, kiddos, looks like I'm stuck," he said.

"Are we near the zoo?" asked Annie.

"It's still a long ways from here, I'm sorry to say," said the driver. "But this taxi's not going anywhere. I don't know what else to tell you."

"Oh. Well, thanks," said Annie. "How much do we owe you?"

"Forget it, kiddo," said the driver. "Good luck!"

"Good luck yourself, kiddo," said Annie. She opened the door, and she and Jack climbed out into the cold wind. The taxi motor kept running, but the wheels only spun in place, sending up sprays of dirty snow.

"I don't believe this," said Jack.

"Maybe there's a subway station somewhere near here," said Annie.

"The man in the booth said the subways aren't running all the way to the zoo," said Jack.

"I know, but maybe we can at least get closer," said Annie.

Jack and Annie struggled through the storm until they came to a steep cliff. Over the edge of the cliff they saw nothing but a cloud of wind-blown snow.

"Where are we?" said Annie.

"I have no idea," said Jack. His teeth chattered. His eyes and ears stung with the cold, and his hands and feet felt numb. *Isn't this what frostbite feels like?* he thought. *Numb?*

"Let's go back and sit in that taxi until we figure out what to do," said Jack. "At least get out of the wind."

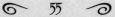

"Okay," said Annie. "Maybe the driver will get it going again."

Jack and Annie headed back the way they'd come. But the taxi was gone!

"Hey, he must've got unstuck!" said Annie. "And he left us!"

"Oh, man," said Jack. "We're having really rotten luck. And I think I'm starting to get frostbite. Seriously."

"It looks like there's a building over there," said Annie. "I see a tower."

"Yeah, me too," said Jack. "Let's go there and try to figure out what to do next."

Jack and Annie trekked up what looked like a long driveway until they came to the gray stone building. Jack wiped snow from a sign in front.

CLOISTERS OF THE METROPOLITAN MUSEUM, OPEN TO THE PUBLIC

"A museum!" said Annie. "Let's go in and ask them how to get to the zoo."

"Yeah, and get warm for a minute," said Jack.

He and Annie climbed the snow-covered steps of the Cloisters. Annie opened the door, and the wind nearly swept them inside.

They pushed the door shut.

"Ah! My first visitors all day!" a woman chirped.

Jack and Annie turned around. A museum lady sat at a desk in a corner. Dressed in a green uniform, she was tall and thin with a friendly face and short gray hair.

"I'm sorry, but we can't stay long," said Annie. "We just came here to get warm for a minute and get some information."

"What can I tell you?" the woman asked.

"We're trying to get to the Bronx Zoo," said Jack. "Is there a subway near here?"

"Well, the A train is close by," said the museum lady. "But that won't take you anywhere near the zoo."

"Oh, darn," said Annie.

"Oh, I wouldn't be so sad," the woman said

brightly. "If I were you, I'd stay right here and enjoy the Cloisters! You won't regret it, I promise. The Cloisters holds most of the medieval collection of the world-famous Metropolitan Museum of Art."

"What's a cloister?" Annie asked.

"It's an enclosed garden or courtyard," said the museum lady. "We have four in all. They beautifully evoke medieval times, from the Romanesque period to the light, airy elegance of the Gothic."

"Cool," said Jack politely. He had no idea what she was talking about.

"I suppose the gardens *are* cool most days, my dear," said the woman. "But today they are freezing! Never mind, you don't have to spend time in the gardens to enjoy the museum. Inside, we have many beautiful exhibits. The tapestries are especially lovely. They were woven with beautiful yarns by weavers from the Netherlands. For years, they hung in a French castle and managed to escape destruction during the Revolution. Then, for two generations—"

"Excuse me," said Jack. He was eager to end the woman's boring lecture so they could be on their way.

But she kept talking excitedly. "The tapestries were used by peasants to protect potatoes stored in their barns until, eventually, a countess rescued them. They were restored, and in 1922, Mr. John D. Rockefeller, Jr., bought them. Just last year, Mr. Rockefeller gave them as gifts to—"

"Oh, that is so cool!" interrupted Jack loudly. He pretended to be interested so they could escape. "We'd *love* to see them! Where are they?"

"The tapestry room is just on the other side of the first cloister," the woman said, pointing. "Turn that corner, go out the door, and then walk through the garden to the door of the tapestry room."

"Let's go, Annie. Quick!" said Jack. He and Annie went around the corner, out the door, and into a snowy garden.

"Whew!" said Jack. "I didn't want to be rude. But we're short on time."

"I know," said Annie.

"What now?" said Jack, shivering in the cold.

"We need to figure out exactly where we are," said Annie, "and where the Bronx Zoo is. Maybe we can just walk there from here."

"Come on, let's get inside the tapestry room and check our research book for a map," said Jack.

They walked along the edge of the garden under a covered walkway. When they came to a door, Jack pushed it open, and he and Annie slipped out of the cold into a large, warm room.

Jack closed the door against the storm and unbuckled his briefcase to take out their research book.

"Ohh . . . wow!" breathed Annie.

"What? What?" said Jack. He looked up.

The walls of the room were covered with cloth hangings—tapestries shimmering with gold and silver.

"Oh . . . !" whispered Jack.

"A *unicorn*!" said Annie.

CHAPTER SIX

The Hunt of the Unicorn

There were seven tapestries in all. Each was almost as high as the wooden ceiling. Jack read aloud from a sign on the wall under the first one:

> **The Hunt of the Unicorn**
> **Tapestries woven in the Netherlands**
> **at the end of the 1400s**

The first tapestry showed hunters and hounds searching for the unicorn. The second showed the unicorn being found.

The other tapestries showed the unicorn trying to escape, leaping from a stream, chased by hounds, then captured and slain by the hunters' spears.

Oddly, the last tapestry showed the unicorn alive again. He was sitting in a garden of flowers surrounded by a wooden fence. There was a wide blue and gold collar around his neck, and he was chained to a tree.

"That's *him*," Annie said softly.

"How can it be him?" said Jack. "He's a picture in a tapestry."

"Read Merlin's poem again," said Annie.

Jack unbuckled his briefcase and pulled out the parchment scroll. He read aloud.

> *The very last unicorn*
> *Is now hidden well*
> *By those who have put him*
> *Under a spell.*

"The unicorn is hidden in the tapestry," said Annie. "The people who wove it must be the ones who put him under a spell."

"Hmm . . . ," said Jack. He read on.

Four centuries, four decades
From that afternoon,
At the end of November,
Before the blue moon . . .

"Stop, do the math," said Annie.

"Right," said Jack. He took out his notebook and pencil. "Okay, four centuries is four hundred, and four decades is forty. Add 'em up, you get four hundred forty. Then if you subtract four hundred forty from 1938, you get . . . 1498."

"It works!" said Annie. "The sign says the tapestries were woven at the end of the 1400s! And it's the end of November, and Mr. Perkins said there's a blue moon tonight!"

"Oh, man," whispered Jack. He kept reading.

He will wake once more
And be free to go home
If you call out his name:
Divine Flower of Rome.

Annie looked up at the tapestry. *"Divine Flower!"* she called.

Nothing happened.

"*Divine Flower of Rome!*" Jack called.

Jack and Annie watched and waited. Nothing changed in the tapestry. It looked exactly the same.

"Maybe he's not the right unicorn after all," said Jack.

"Maybe it's just not the right name," said Annie. "Read the rest."

Jack read more of the poem.

> *You must coax him to stand*
> *Once his name is spoken.*
> *His chain will break*
> *And the spell, too, be broken.*

"He *is* the right unicorn!" said Annie. "See? There's the chain!" She pointed to the chain in the last tapestry.

"Yeah, but why didn't calling his name work?" said Jack. "Why didn't he wake up?"

"I don't know," said Annie. "What else does the poem say?"

Jack read on.

> *Then a young girl must love him*
> *And show him the way,*
> *Lest he be trapped forever*
> *On public display.*
>
> *If he loses this chance*
> *To rise and depart,*
> *All magic will fade*
> *From his horn and his heart.*

"He *is* on public display, and *I'm* the girl, Jack!" said Annie. "I love him a lot! I'll show him the way!"

"Okay, calm down. First we need to wake him up," said Jack.

Voices came from outside. Jack moved to a window. He looked out into the courtyard. Two people were coming through the cloister, their heads down against the flying snow. One wore a dark cape, and the other a tan raincoat.

Jack turned back to Annie, a big grin on his face. "You were right! They found us! Teddy and

Kathleen are here!" he said. "*They'll* know how to break the spell!"

"Of course!" said Annie, beaming. "Quick, let's hide and surprise *them* for a change."

"In there!" said Jack. He and Annie hurried into a long room off the tapestry room. They heard the door from the cloister open. They felt a rush of cold air. They heard footsteps.

Jack and Annie grinned at each other. Jack put his finger to his lips. Then a quick, nervous boy's voice came from the tapestry room: "Grinda, they are not here!"

"I see that, Balor, but *look*—"

"Ahh! Is it *him*, Grinda?"

Annie grabbed Jack's arm. "Balor? Grinda?" she whispered.

"Shh," whispered Jack.

"Of course 'tis him!" said the girl. "I told you those Frog Creek brats would lead us to him! Get the rope ready!"

"Aye," said the boy.

Jack and Annie carefully peeked around the

corner. They saw a girl and boy standing with their backs to them, facing the unicorn in the last tapestry. The boy held a thick black rope.

"Call out his name, Grinda," said the boy.

The girl took a step toward the tapestry. She raised her arms in front of the unicorn. *"Dianthus!"* she called.

Wind whistled through the open doorway. The flowers in the tapestry swayed as if the wind were blowing them. The scent of roses wafted through the room. The unicorn moved his head.

"Ohh!" whispered Annie.

"Get ready, Balor, to take him back to the Master," said the girl.

Annie clutched Jack's arm. "Who's the Master?" she whispered.

"I don't know," whispered Jack. "But I don't think he's a good guy."

The girl turned back to the tapestry and spoke softly to the unicorn. "Come, come, my lovely Dianthus, stand up now. Come out of that old rug. . . ."

The unicorn turned his head and looked out at the girl. The look in his blue eyes was ancient yet young, wise yet innocent. He lifted his head as if he were about to stand.

The girl nodded to the boy. The boy slowly coiled the black rope into a noose. The girl looked at the unicorn again. "Come to me, Dianthus!" she coaxed. "Don't be afraid. I'll love you and show you the way—"

"No, Dianthus!" yelled Annie. "Don't go to her!" Annie and Jack bolted from their hiding place.

Balor and Grinda whirled around in surprise. They both had pale faces and pale shining eyes.

"Leave him alone!" Annie yelled at the strange pair. "You don't love him! *We* love him!"

At that moment, there was a flash of light, and the unicorn in the tapestry leapt like a deer over the woven fence. Balor and Grinda shrieked and jumped back. Jack covered his head.

Then there was silence. Jack looked up. The tapestry on the wall was unchanged—it still showed a unicorn woven from yarn chained to a tree.

But standing on the floor of the museum was the most beautiful creature Jack had ever seen.

CHAPTER SEVEN

Dianthus

The unicorn had a broad milk-white chest and graceful neck. A tuft of hair curled under his chin. A long, spiraled horn rose from the middle of his forehead. He stood very still and very tall. His whole body seemed to be glowing.

Balor and Grinda just stared at him. They both looked frightened. But Annie stepped forward. "Hi, Dianthus," she whispered. She reached out and gently touched the unicorn's white chest. "Feel, Jack, feel his heart pounding."

"Move away!" ordered Grinda. The girl stepped

between Jack and Annie. "He is ours and he is coming with us."

"He's *not* yours!" said Annie.

"Who *are* you, anyway?" said Jack. "Where did you come from?"

Grinda glared at Jack. "We come from the same magic world *he* comes from," she said. "He belongs with us, not *you*. Balor!"

The boy shoved Annie aside and tried to loop the black rope around the unicorn's neck. But Dianthus reared up and wheeled around, forcing Balor and Grinda out of his way.

Dianthus leapt across the tapestry room toward the garden. Jack and Annie followed him through the open doorway into the snowy cloister. Balor and Grinda charged after them. They pushed past Jack and Annie to Dianthus. Balor grabbed the unicorn's blue collar. "You are coming with us, stupid, like it or not!"

"Don't pull on him!" yelled Annie. "And don't call him stupid!"

Dianthus tried to back up.

"Let go!" screamed Annie. "He doesn't want to go with you!"

"He has no choice," said Grinda. "As soon as that rope goes around his neck, all three of us will be instantly transported back to the Castle of the Dark Wizard."

"No!" Jack shouted. He charged at Balor and tried to grab the rope from his hand. Balor let go of the unicorn's collar and shoved Jack into the snow. Then he turned back to the unicorn and began to swing the magic rope like a lasso.

Dianthus reared up again and kicked his legs. Breath from his nostrils billowed into the icy air.

"A rhyme, Jack!" yelled Annie. "A rhyme!"

Kneeling in the snow, Jack yanked the book from his briefcase. He frantically turned the pages, looking for a rhyme they hadn't used. *"Call a Cloud from the Sky?"* he shouted to Annie.

"Anything!" she called. "Try it!"

Jack read the rhyme aloud:

Down from high, out of the sky,
Ee-no-fain-ee-ro-lie!

A thick white fog instantly filled the cloister. The fog was so dense that Jack couldn't even see his own hand.

"Balor, where are you?" shrieked Grinda.

"Here!" the boy yelled.

Someone grabbed Jack. He struggled to break free. "Let me go!" he shouted.

"It's me!" whispered Annie. "Come on!"

Jack stood up, clinging to Annie. They stumbled together through the garden. Feeling their way along the walkway, they came to the door that led to the main hall.

"Dianthus, here!" Annie whispered.

Jack heard the soft crunch of the unicorn's hooves in the frozen snow.

"Where did he go?" Balor shouted.

"Find him!" yelled Grinda.

Jack reached out and felt the unicorn's soft mane. Annie pushed open the door. Then she, Dianthus, and Jack slipped inside the main hall.

Jack closed the door before Balor and Grinda could escape the garden. There wasn't a wisp of fog in the main hall. The museum lady was still behind her desk. She stared at Jack, Annie, and the glowing unicorn that had just come in from the garden. Her mouth opened, and then closed.

Dianthus stepped lightly over the wooden floor. Jack and Annie followed him.

The museum lady never blinked. As Dianthus walked gracefully past her desk, she reached out and touched him. She gasped and quickly drew back her hand.

"Thanks for keeping the museum open today," said Annie. "And thank Mr. Rockefeller for his gifts."

The museum lady opened and closed her mouth again, still unable to speak.

Jack opened the door that led to the street. Jack and Annie followed Dianthus out of the museum and down the stone steps. The blizzard had gotten much worse. Snow was coming down harder than ever. The wind was wailing. The unicorn shook his head and knelt down.

"He wants us to get on his back!" said Annie. "Quick! Climb on behind me!" Annie climbed onto the unicorn's back. Jack climbed on behind her.

Dianthus stood up to his full height.

Grinda and Balor burst out the door of the museum. "Stop!" screamed Grinda.

Dianthus looked back at them. Then he leapt nimbly over a snowdrift and headed into the darkening storm.

CHAPTER EIGHT

Back to Life

Jack clung to Annie. Dianthus cleared the driveway of the Cloisters and began to run with ease down the street. His long strides were so light and graceful, Jack could hardly feel the movement.

As the unicorn ran, he held his head high. His long, spiraled horn pierced the raging storm, seeming to calm the winds and snow. Jack realized he could feel his fingers and toes again. His whole body began to feel warm.

Dianthus headed down a deserted parkway along the waterfront, past an empty bridge. The bridge's towers and cables formed a silver arc over a wide river. Whitecaps swept across the water's surface. As the unicorn trotted past the river, the water became still.

Dianthus left the riverside and headed down a city street. The wind whistled between tall buildings, blowing the snow into great drifts. But the unicorn's horn turned the howling wind into a soft breeze. The wild blowing snow became floating, star-shaped flakes, like the snowflakes on Christmas cards.

As the unicorn trotted down the street, snow-bound taxis and streetcars started moving again. Lights came on in cafés and jazz clubs. Jack heard happy music coming from inside.

With a calm, steady trot, the unicorn pranced on through the city. As he moved past old mansions, broken-down tenements, and shabby hotels, people peeked out of doorways and windows to see why the sounds of the storm had died away. When they caught sight of Dianthus, with his horn shining in the windless air, they broke into joyful smiles. Church bells started ringing through the white silence.

Finally Dianthus came to a stone wall bordering Central Park. He jumped over the wall and landed knee-deep in a heap of snow. The unicorn leapt effortlessly out of the drift and cantered over a field and down a slope.

Slowly the clouds parted, and light from the setting sun poured down.

"Hot corn!" a peddler shouted, plowing his pushcart through the snow.

"Roasted chestnuts!" shouted another.

The good smells of the corn and nuts filled the

crisp golden air of the park. The unicorn trotted past Belvedere Castle. Bill Perkins stood outside, staring up at the clear blue sky.

"Hey, Mr. Perkins, the monster storm's not coming!" shouted Annie.

The weatherman saw Jack and Annie on the back of the white unicorn. His jaw dropped. Then he smiled and waved.

Jack and Annie rode on. When they passed the statue of the winged angel, Jack thought he saw her move her great wings. "Did you see that?" he cried.

"Yes!" said Annie.

When they passed the statue of Balto, Jack heard the sled dog bark.

When they rode past the merry-go-round, Jack heard a chorus of neighs and whinnies accompanied by lively carousel music.

Dianthus pranced down a shimmering pathway. He leapt over a stone wall and cantered over another field.

The unicorn's horn glistened, and the snowy field reflected gold and copper light. Not until the unicorn came to the tree that held the tree house did he stop.

Annie hugged the unicorn's long, graceful neck. "Thank you, thank you!" she whispered, and kissed him.

"Yeah, wow," breathed Jack.

Annie looked at Jack over her shoulder. "What now?" she asked.

"I guess we climb off," said Jack.

"But then what?" Annie asked sadly. "Where does he go?"

"That's a good question," said Jack.

"He comes with us, of course," someone said.

Jack and Annie gasped.

Balor and Grinda slunk out from behind the tree. Balor carried the black rope.

Jack was stunned. "How—how did you get here so fast?" he asked.

"We took the A train," said Balor. "'Tis actually

85

a bit faster than riding a unicorn." The boy laughed meanly.

"Shut up, Balor," said Grinda. Then she turned to Jack and Annie. "I am glad you had a happy little ride. But you can say good-bye to Dianthus now. We will take him from here."

"No, you won't!" said Annie.

"Stay away from us!" said Jack.

"Come on, Dianthus, let's go!" said Annie.

Before Dianthus could move, Grinda rushed forward and grabbed his collar with both hands. The unicorn snorted and shook his head. Grinda clung fiercely to the collar. "Get the rope over his head, Balor!" she yelled. "Now!"

Balor looped the black rope into a noose again. The unicorn twisted and turned his head.

Jack kicked at Balor. "Stop!" he yelled. "Get away from us!" Jack felt stupid just yelling and kicking, but he didn't know what else to do.

As Balor and Grinda struggled to get the noose over the unicorn's head, Annie pointed at them. In a loud voice, she shouted:

Fowl of air, appear now here!
Aka-aka-aka-mere!

The black rope fell to the snow. Balor and Grinda started to spin around. They spun like two spinning tops. As they spun, they grew smaller and smaller. Jack saw a blur of colors: gray and brown, green and white, a dash of orange, a dash of yellow.

The spinning slowly came to a stop. The two scary teenagers were gone. In their place were two small mallard ducks.

CHAPTER NINE

It's *Them!*

One duck was gray with black and white markings. The other had a glossy green head and a rust-colored chest. Both had orange webbed feet and long yellow bills. *Quack, quack,* they said.

Annie looked over her shoulder at Jack. "I memorized the duck rhyme a while ago," she said with a grin. "I knew it would come in handy someday."

Jack laughed. "Good work," he said.

The two ducks waddled around on their bright orange feet, quacking. Answering cries came from overhead. A flock of ducks was flying through the clear November sky.

"Go on, Balor and Grinda!" Annie shouted to the two mallards. "Go with them now!"

The mallards quacked at Annie.

"Go on!" Jack chimed in. "Fly south for the winter! You'll have fun! We promise!"

The two mallards quacked and flapped their wings. First one and then the other rose off the ground. They flew high into the sky. Jack held his breath as he watched the mallards soar away, flying south over New York City.

Annie put her arms around the unicorn's neck. Then she rested her head on his silky white mane. "You're safe now," she said. "But you have to leave us. I have to show you the way to Camelot. The problem is, I don't know how to do that."

AH-U-GA! AH-U-GA!

Jack looked over at an avenue that bordered the park. A big yellow taxi was parked by the curb. The driver was honking his horn. He waved through the window.

"What's that guy want?" said Annie, sitting up.

"I don't know," said Jack.

The driver jumped out of the car. He wore a cap and a plaid scarf. "Hey, it's the same driver who deserted us outside the Cloisters," said Annie.

The passenger door of the taxi opened, and a girl stepped out. She was wearing a purple shawl. "And that's the girl who told us to get off at the wrong subway stop," said Jack.

The taxi driver and the girl in the shawl both waved at Jack and Annie. Then the driver lifted his cap and pulled down his scarf. He had red curly hair and a wonderfully familiar grin.

The girl pulled the shawl off her head. Beautiful long black curls fell down to her waist.

"It's *them*!" said Jack.

"Teddy! Kathleen!" Annie shouted.

Jack and Annie slid off the unicorn's back onto

the snowy ground. The young enchanters ran across the snow to them. Annie threw her arms around Teddy. Kathleen threw her arms around Jack. The four of them laughed and talked at the same time.

"That was *you!*"

"That was *you!*"

"That was *us!*"

"I'm sorry I told you to get off at the wrong stop," said Kathleen. "But Teddy was waiting for you there!"

"And I'm sorry I left you stranded in the storm," said Teddy. "But I knew you'd find your way to the Cloisters!"

"We thought you guys were these two kids following us, Balor and Grinda!" said Annie.

"Yes, we just saw you turn them into ducks!" said Kathleen. "Brilliant!"

"Who were they?" asked Jack.

"Apprentices of the Dark Wizard," said Kathleen. "We didn't know they were following you! Even *Merlin* didn't know."

"They were pretty creepy," said Jack.

"Yeah, but they actually helped us without meaning to," said Annie. "They knew the unicorn's name."

"We thought it was *Divine Flower of Rome*," said Jack.

"I told Merlin that clue might be a bit difficult," said Teddy. "Divine Flower is *dianthus* in Latin, the language of old Rome."

"So do Grinda and Balor know Latin?" asked Annie.

"Hardly," said Teddy. "The unicorn's name is famous throughout the Otherworld. He is known for his great magic."

"And for his goodness," added Kathleen.

"We know about his goodness," said Annie. "When he ran through the streets with his horn in the air, the blizzard ended. And everyone we passed cheered up and seemed to get more hopeful."

"The Dark Wizard was trying to capture Dianthus so he could keep the unicorn's good magic from the rest of the world," said Kathleen. "Merlin will be very pleased that you have foiled the wizard's plan."

"In truth, I believe he would like to thank you himself," said Teddy. He turned toward the yellow taxi parked by the curb.

The back door of the car opened, and two grown-ups stepped out: a tall, elegant woman wearing a wine-colored cloak and a man in a dark blue robe. The man had a long white beard. The woman had long white hair.

"Morgan! Merlin!" whispered Jack.

As the wizard and magical librarian of Camelot walked across the snow, Dianthus stepped forward to greet them. He bowed his head. Merlin tenderly stroked the unicorn's white neck.

Morgan le Fay turned to Jack and Annie. "Hello," she said, smiling. "It is good to see you both." Her lovely voice washed over Jack like music.

"You too," said Annie, hugging the enchantress.

"What are you and Merlin doing here?" Jack asked.

"I have always wanted to visit New York City," said Morgan. "Teddy has just given us quite a ride in that taxi. Merlin had to tell him to slow down several times." Morgan laughed and turned toward Merlin.

"Quite a ride indeed," said Merlin. "Greetings to you both, Jack and Annie."

"Greetings," they said.

"Thank you for saving my beloved Dianthus," said Merlin. "Long ago, he was stolen from Camelot by evildoers. He was rescued by magic weavers in the Netherlands. To keep him safe, they used their art to hide him in their tapestries. I knew I could entrust you two to set him free on the day the spell was to end. But your mission turned out to be more dangerous than I intended. I did not know the Dark Wizard had sent his apprentices to follow you and capture the unicorn."

"Poor Grinda and Balor," said Annie. "Now they're ducks."

"Oh, do not worry," said Teddy. "The spell will wear off in a few days, and they'll find their way home."

"Yes," said Kathleen, "and I am sure the Dark Wizard will have some other wicked plan for them."

"Aye," said Merlin, "but they will no longer have the use of their black rope." He picked the rope up from the ground and handed it to Teddy.

"Take this back to Camelot and see that it is destroyed."

"Gladly," said Teddy.

"It must be terrible to work for the Dark Wizard," said Annie. She looked at Merlin. "I'm glad we work for you instead."

Merlin smiled. "And so am I," he said. "On your last four missions, you and Jack have proved you know how to use magic wisely. And for that, I now entrust you with one of Camelot's greatest treasures."

Merlin pulled a spiraled wand from his robe. "I give you the Wand of Dianthus," he said. "As you can see, the wand is made in the shape of the unicorn's horn. It has a bit of his magic in it." Merlin held the silver wand out to Jack and Annie.

Jack took the wand from Merlin. It burned in his hand—with cold or warmth, he couldn't tell which.

"With the help of the wand, you can make your own magic," said Merlin.

"But you can only use it after you have tried your hardest," said Morgan, "and remember that it can only be used for another's good."

"We'll remember," breathed Annie.

"Thank you," said Jack. He unbuckled his briefcase and carefully placed the silver wand inside.

"We must leave you now," said Merlin. He turned to Teddy and Kathleen. "You may ride Dianthus home to Camelot. I will be along shortly. But first, I would like to drive that taxi around New York City myself. Morgan, will you join me?"

"Indeed," said Morgan. "But drive a bit more slowly than Teddy, please."

"I promise nothing," said Merlin. He looked

at Jack and Annie. "Good evening to you, my friends. I will call for you again soon."

"Bye," said Annie and Jack.

Merlin took Morgan's arm, and the two walked back to the taxi and climbed into the front seat. The big yellow car sputtered and then took off wildly. As it careened up the avenue, Merlin blew its horn.

AH-U-GA! AH-U-GA!

CHAPTER TEN

The Wand of Dianthus

Jack, Annie, Teddy, and Kathleen laughed.

"My," said Kathleen. "I believe I would much rather ride Dianthus than go with Merlin!"

The white unicorn knelt in the snow. Kathleen and Teddy climbed onto his back. Dianthus stood up.

Teddy smiled down at Jack and Annie. "You know 'tis a very great honor to be given the Wand of Dianthus," he said.

"I know," said Jack shyly. "Thanks for getting us to the right place at the right time today."

"Hey, were you guys in Venice, looking out for us there, too?" said Annie. "And Baghdad? And Paris?"

The two young enchanters looked at one another. Then they nodded their heads.

"We knew it!" said Annie. "Thanks for helping us!"

"And thanks for the book of magic rhymes," said Jack.

"You are most welcome," said Teddy. "And now we must go. We hope to see you again soon."

"Good-bye, Dianthus," said Annie. She stroked the unicorn's neck one last time.

Dianthus lowered his head and stared at her with his soft blue eyes. They sparkled in the last bit of daylight. Annie stood on her toes and whispered in the unicorn's ear. Then she stepped back.

Dianthus snorted. He raised his head. Then he leapt forward. In a flash of silver, the unicorn and his two riders were gone.

Standing in the cold dusk, Annie stared silently into the distance.

"What did you say to him?" asked Jack.

"I told him he had to go with Teddy and Kathleen," Annie said. She blinked back tears. "I told him they would show him the way home now."

"Oh," said Jack. He put his hand on Annie's back. "Don't worry. We'll see Dianthus again someday. I just feel it."

Annie smiled. "You're starting to sound like me," she said.

"Uh-oh," said Jack. He shivered. Night was falling fast. "Ready?"

"Sure, let's go," said Annie. She followed Jack to the tree house and up the rope ladder. They climbed inside and looked out the window.

The lights of New York City were starting to come on. A full moon was rising over the snow-covered park.

"Hello, blue moon," said Jack.

"Good-bye, blue moon," said Annie.

Jack picked up the scroll from Merlin. He pointed to the words *Frog Creek* in Merlin's note. "I wish we could go home!" he said.

The wind started to blow.

The tree house started to spin.

It spun faster and faster.

Then everything was still.

Absolutely still.

❋ ❋ ❋

A cold wind blew through the Frog Creek woods. A few fat snowflakes drifted into the tree house. Jack and Annie were dressed in their own clothes again. Jack's briefcase had turned back into a backpack.

Jack quickly opened the pack and looked inside. "Good," he said. "The Wand of Dianthus is still there."

"Should we take it home with us?" asked Annie.

"I think so," said Jack. "We can keep it safe

until our next mission." He pulled Teddy and Kathleen's book of rhymes out of his pack.

"I guess we can keep our book of rhymes as a souvenir," Jack said. "We won't be using it anymore since we've used up all the rhymes." He stuffed the book back into his backpack.

"We haven't used *all* of them," said Annie. "We still have one left, remember? *Find a Treasure You Must Never Lose.*"

"Oh, I already used that one," said Jack. "Come on, let's go." He grabbed his pack and started down the rope ladder.

"What do you mean you already used that one?" Annie said as she followed him down. "When did you use *that* rhyme?"

Jack stepped onto the ground. "How do you think I found you when you got lost in Central Park?" he said.

"Wait, you thought *I* was a treasure?" said Annie.

Jack shrugged. "I guess," he said. "At least today I did."

Annie smiled. "Cool," she said. "Thanks for finding me when you got lost."

"Not me, *you*," said Jack. "You're the one who got lost."

"No, *you*," said Annie.

"*You*," said Jack.

"Youyouyouyouyou!" said Annie.

Jack laughed. "Whatever," he said. "Let's go have some of Dad's hot chocolate."

The snow began to fall harder. As the cold wind rattled the bare trees of the Frog Creek woods, Jack and Annie hurried home.

More Facts for Jack and Annie and You!

The Great Depression: Today, older New Yorkers remember the Great Depression as one of the most difficult times in the city's history. Lasting from 1929 to about 1939, the Depression was a time when all of America, as well as much of Europe, suffered terrible economic problems that caused many people to lose their jobs.

Subways: Today, millions of people ride the New York subways every day. There are over 400 miles of tracks. Riders no longer drop coins or tokens into a slot in the turnstiles, though. They now slide a MetroCard through an electronic card reader.

Central Park: Today, more than 250,000 people might visit Central Park on a warm weekend and picnic, jog, skate, bicycle, listen to music, or walk dogs. Designed over 150 years ago, Central Park was the first major park created entirely for public use. Its designers, Frederick Law Olmsted and Calvert Vaux, believed that nature could lift the spirits of city dwellers and bring together people from all walks of life.

Belvedere Castle: Today, Belvedere Castle in Central Park serves as a nature observatory. If you live in New York City, you have often heard on TV or radio: "The temperature in Central Park is . . . " That information is coming from the weather instruments that are still housed in the castle.

John D. Rockefeller: Today, America remembers John D. Rockefeller as once being the richest man in the country. After founding the Standard Oil Company, he focused on giving away half of his fortune. Through the generosity of his son, John D. Rockefeller, Jr., a small museum in Fort Tryon Park in the northern part of the city was acquired by the Metropolitan Museum of Art. That museum is known as the Cloisters.

The Cloisters: Today, the Cloisters is filled with approximately 5,000 works of medieval art, including many works from Rockefeller's own medieval art collection, such as the famous Unicorn Tapestries.

Unicorns: Today, unicorns appear in old stories from countries all over the world, most notably China, India, and medieval Europe. There is no proof that unicorns ever actually existed, though. The only land animal with a single horn is a rhinoceros.

Illustrator's Note

I have illustrated all the Magic Tree House books, but illustrating *Blizzard of the Blue Moon* has been the most enjoyable so far.

My research for this project brought back many fond memories because as a student I often visited many of the places mentioned in the story, especially in Central Park, where I loved to sketch.

Since I still live close to New York City, I came to the city several times and followed the same route that Jack and Annie took from Central Park to the Cloisters.

Many of the places in the story are not very

different than they were in 1938, and I was able to sketch and photograph them. The taxis and the subway trains have changed, but I was able to find pictures of these in books.

Turn the page for great activities!

Fun Activities for Jack and Annie and *You*!

Puzzle of the Blue Moon

Jack and Annie learned many new things on their adventure in 1938 New York City. Did you?

Put your knowledge to the test with this puzzle. You can use a notebook or make a copy of this page if you don't want to write in your book.

1. A woven cloth hanging.

☐ ☐ ☐ ○ ☐ ☐ ☐ ☐

2. A famous dog whose statue is in Central Park.

☐ ☐ ○ ☐ ☐

3. The second full moon in a month.

☐ ☐ ☐ ☐ ☐ ☐ ○ ☐

4. In New York City in the 1930s, these yellow cars had a checkerboard stripe.

○ ☐ ☐ ☐ ☐

5. The name of the castle in Central Park.

☐ ☐ ☐ ☐ ☐ ☐ ☐ ◯ ☐

6. A giant snowstorm.

☐ ☐ ◯ ☐ ☐ ☐ ☐ ☐

7. The period of hard times in the 1930s.

☐ ☐ ☐ ☐ ☐

☐ ☐ ☐ ☐ ◯ ☐ ☐ ☐ ☐

8. An 840-acre natural area in New York City with thirty-two miles of footpaths.

◯ ☐ ☐ ☐ ☐ ☐ ☐

☐ ☐ ☐ ☐

Now look at your answers above. The letters that are circled spell a word—but that word is scrambled! Can you unscramble it to spell a word that Jack and Annie learned at the museum in New York City?

Make your own snow globe!

If you like the picture of Jack and Annie riding the unicorn through a snowstorm on the cover of this book, you might want to try making your own snowy scene. Here's a fun way to make a glittery snow globe.

Snow Globe
What you need:
- Clean jar with a lid
- Baby oil
- Small figurines and/or other objects to go in scene
- Glitter and/or white eggshells
- Florist clay
- Glue

Remove the lid from the jar. With the florist clay, attach the figurines and/or other objects to the inside of the lid to form a scene. You could use small plastic toys, beads, plastic plants, or things you made yourself out of modeling clay, foil, or other materials that won't decay or dissolve.

Fill the jar almost to the top with baby oil. Add about a tablespoon of crushed white eggshells, glitter, or a combination of the two.

Put a small amount of glue around the inside edges of the lid. Then carefully turn the lid with your scene on it upside down and screw the lid on the jar tightly. Add some more glue around the edges of the lid to make sure it is sealed tightly. If you have a hot glue gun, you can ask a grownup to help you use it to make a stronger seal around the lid.

Wait until the glue is dry. Then turn the jar over, shake it up, and enjoy your sparkly scene!

A Story in Pictures!

The Hunt of the Unicorn is a famous series of medieval tapestries that is still on display at the Cloisters today. Together, the woven pictures tell a story about capturing a unicorn.

Can you tell a story without using any words? You don't have to know how to weave a tapestry in order to try! Take a few pieces of paper and draw or paint a series of pictures that form a story.

Use your imagination and have fun!

Here's a special preview of
Magic Tree House #37
(A Merlin Mission)
Dragon of the Red Dawn

Jack and Annie go on another amazing
adventure filled with history, magic, and a
legendary dragon!

CHAPTER ONE

For Merlin's Sake

*T*ap, *tap, tap.*

Jack was dreaming that a white bird was pecking at his window. *Tap . . . tap.* A red bird appeared and pecked with the white bird. *Tap . . . tap.*

"Jack, wake up!" said Annie.

Jack opened his eyes.

"They're here!" said Annie.

"Who? The birds?" said Jack.

"No! Teddy and Kathleen!" Annie rushed to the window and waved outside. "They're tossing pebbles at our windows."

"Teddy and Kathleen!" Jack jumped out of bed and joined Annie at the window.

The two young enchanters of Camelot were standing in Jack and Annie's front yard. They were dressed in long, dark cloaks. They smiled and waved up at Jack and Annie.

"Merlin must have sent them!" said Jack.

Teddy made a walking motion with his fingers and pointed toward the Frog Creek woods.

Annie nodded eagerly. "They want us to meet them at the tree house!" she said to Jack. "Hurry and get dressed! Before Mom and Dad wake up!"

Annie started out of Jack's room. When she got to the door, she turned. "Oh, and don't forget to bring the Wand of Dianthus!"

Jack threw on his clothes. He grabbed his backpack and peeked inside. The wand was there. Jack put his pack on his back. Then he slipped quietly downstairs and out the door.

Annie was standing on the front porch. "Let's go!" she said.

Jack and Annie ran across their yard and dashed up the sidewalk.

"I wonder why they came for us!" said Annie.

"I wonder where we're going!" said Jack.

"I wonder *everything*!" said Annie.

Jack and Annie crossed the street and hurried into the Frog Creek woods. The early-March trees looked weary from winter, gray and brown with no leaves on them yet.

"Look—" said Annie, out of breath. "They're waiting for us!"

Jack looked up. Teddy and Kathleen were waving from the window of the magic tree house.

Jack grabbed the rope ladder and started up. Annie followed. When Jack and Annie climbed inside the tree house, they threw their arms around Teddy and Kathleen.

"We're so glad to see you!" cried Annie.

"And we are happy to see you, also," said Kathleen. The sea girl's lovely water-blue eyes sparkled.

"Indeed," said Teddy. "It has been too long."

"What's our mission this time?" asked Jack. "Where's Merlin sending us?"

Teddy glanced at Kathleen. "I fear Merlin does not even know we are here," said Teddy. "We have come not at his bidding, but for his sake."

"What does *that* mean?" asked Jack.

"Merlin is not well," said Kathleen. "He complains that he is getting old and feeble and that life is full of sorrows. He does not eat or sleep."

"Oh, no!" said Annie.

"All of Camelot wishes to help him," said Teddy. "But no one knows quite how."

"What can *we* do to help?" asked Jack.

Teddy picked up a book from the corner of the tree house. "Throughout the ages, people all over the world have sought the secrets of happiness," he said. "Morgan wants you to search for four of these secrets to share with Merlin. She believes that the first one might be found *here*."

Jack took the book from Teddy. He read the title aloud.

"Oh, wow, we've been to Japan before!" said Annie.

"Before we met you," Jack said to Teddy and Kathleen. "We had an adventure with ninjas."

"Yes, Morgan told us," said Teddy. "But she said that on that journey, you visited the country-side. This time you must travel to the capital city."

"Are you guys coming with us?" asked Annie.

"I am afraid not," said Kathleen. "We must return to Camelot now to help Morgan. Since

Merlin has fallen ill, she has taken on much of his work."

"You have the wand, do you not?" asked Teddy.

"Yep," said Jack. He reached into his backpack and took out the Wand of Dianthus. The spiraled wand was shaped like a unicorn's horn.

"With the help of the wand, you will make your own magic," said Teddy.

"That's what Merlin said when he gave it to us," said Annie.

"But he didn't say *how*," said Jack.

"It is very simple," said Teddy. "The wand has three rules. First, it only works for the good of others. The wand can never be used for selfish reasons."

"Second, the wand works only after you have tried your very hardest without its help," said Kathleen. "Do not attempt to use its magic too quickly."

"And third, the wand only works with a command of five words," said Teddy. "So you must choose your words carefully."

"Can we review all that, please?" asked Jack.

"Don't worry, I've got it," said Annie. "We have to go. We have to help Merlin as soon as we can."

"If the tree house takes us to Japan, how will you go back to Camelot?" Jack asked Teddy and Kathleen.

Teddy and Kathleen held up their hands. They each wore a sparkling blue ring. "Our magic rings will take us home," said Kathleen.

"And this book from Camelot's library will bring *you* back home to Frog Creek," said Teddy, "after you have completed your mission." He picked up another book lying in a corner. It was the book about Pennsylvania that Jack and Annie had used on their first magic tree house adventures.

"Thanks," said Jack.

"Good-bye," said Annie. "Take good care of Merlin."

"We will try," said Kathleen. She and Teddy raised their magic rings to their lips. They whispered words too softly for Jack and Annie to hear, then blew on the rings. As they blew, the young sorcerers began to fade into the cool morning air. In a moment, they had disappeared completely.

Silence filled the tree house.

Annie turned to Jack. "Ready?" she said.

Jack nodded. He pointed to the cover of the Japan book. "I wish we could go *there*!" he said.

The tree house started to spin.

It spun faster and faster.

Then everything was still.

Absolutely still.

Discover the facts
behind the fiction with the

MAGIC TREE HOUSE®
RESEARCH GUIDES

The must-have, all-true companions for your
favorite Magic Tree House® adventures!

About the Illustrator

Sal Murdocca is best known for his amazing work on the Magic Tree House series. He has written and/or illustrated over two hundred children's books, including *Dancing Granny* by Elizabeth Winthrop, *Double Trouble in Walla Walla* by Andrew Clements, and *Big Numbers* by Edward Packard. He has taught writing and illustration at the Parsons School of Design in New York. He is the librettist for a children's opera and has recently completed his second short film. Sal Murdocca is an avid runner, hiker, and bicyclist. He has often bicycle-toured in Europe and has had many one-man shows of his paintings from these trips. He lives and works with his wife, Nancy, in New City, New York.